THE Cat WANTS Custard

P. Crumble
Lucinda Gifford

SCHOLASTIC

NOW would be good . . .

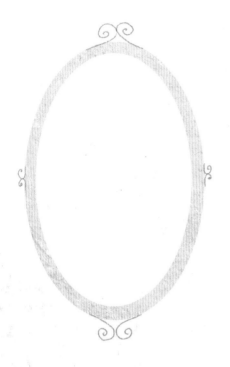

**To AR for discovering that cats
are just like people – PC**

**To Bluey and her family –
Thomas, Spencer and Elliott – LG**

First published in 2016 by Scholastic Australia
An imprint of Scholastic Australia Pty Limited

First published in the UK in 2016 by Scholastic Children's Books
Euston House, 24 Eversholt Street
London NW1 1DB
a division of Scholastic Ltd
www.scholastic.co.uk
London ~ New York ~ Toronto ~ Sydney ~ Auckland
Mexico City ~ New Delhi ~ Hong Kong

Text copyright © 2016 P. Crumble
Illustrations copyright © 2016 Lucinda Gifford

ISBN 978 1407 17410 5

Time for dinner, Kevin.

How about a special treat?

Treat? That's all
you had to say!

Phew. That was tiring!
Get the hint now?

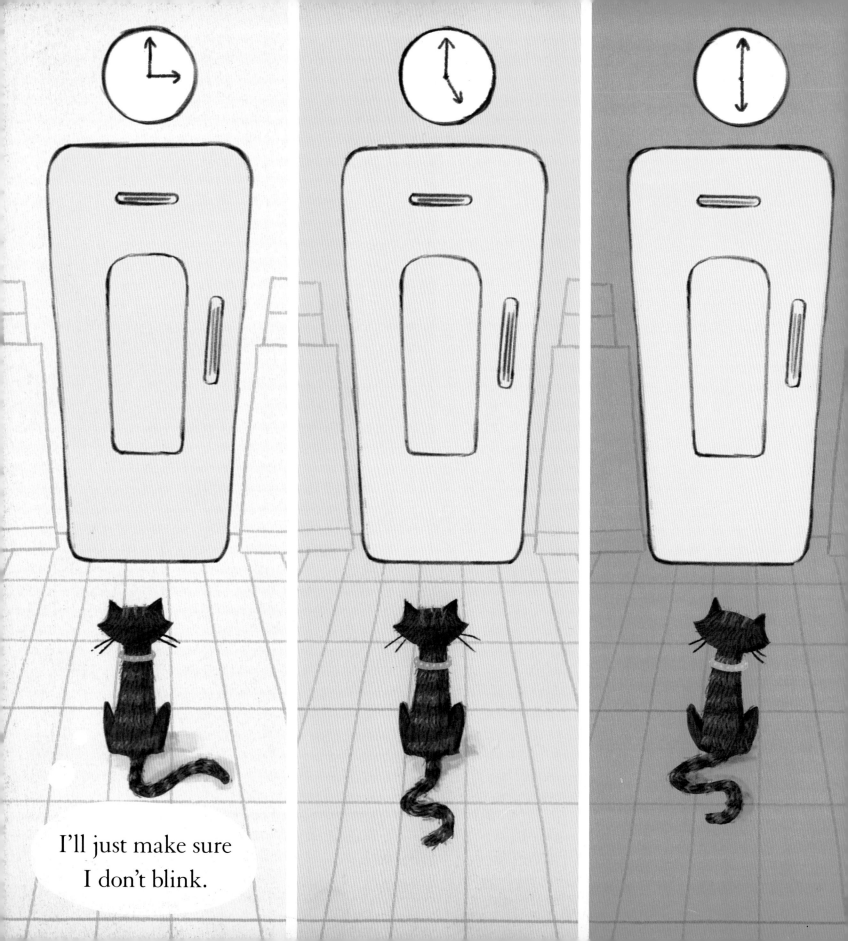

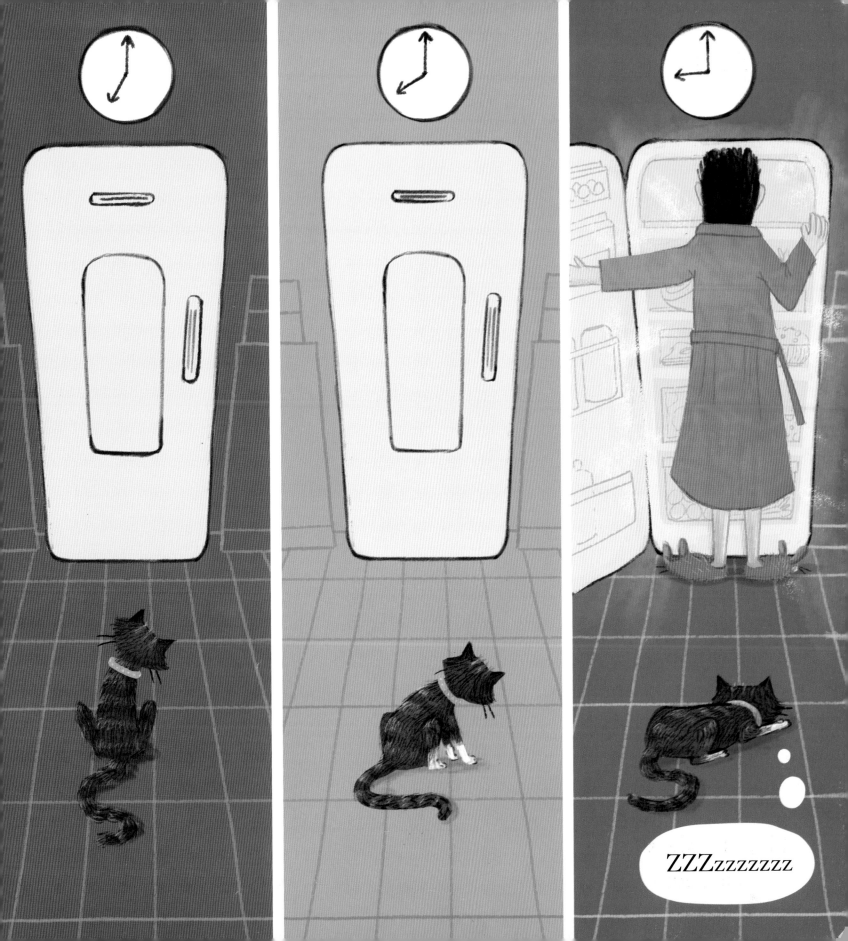

ZZZzzzzzzz

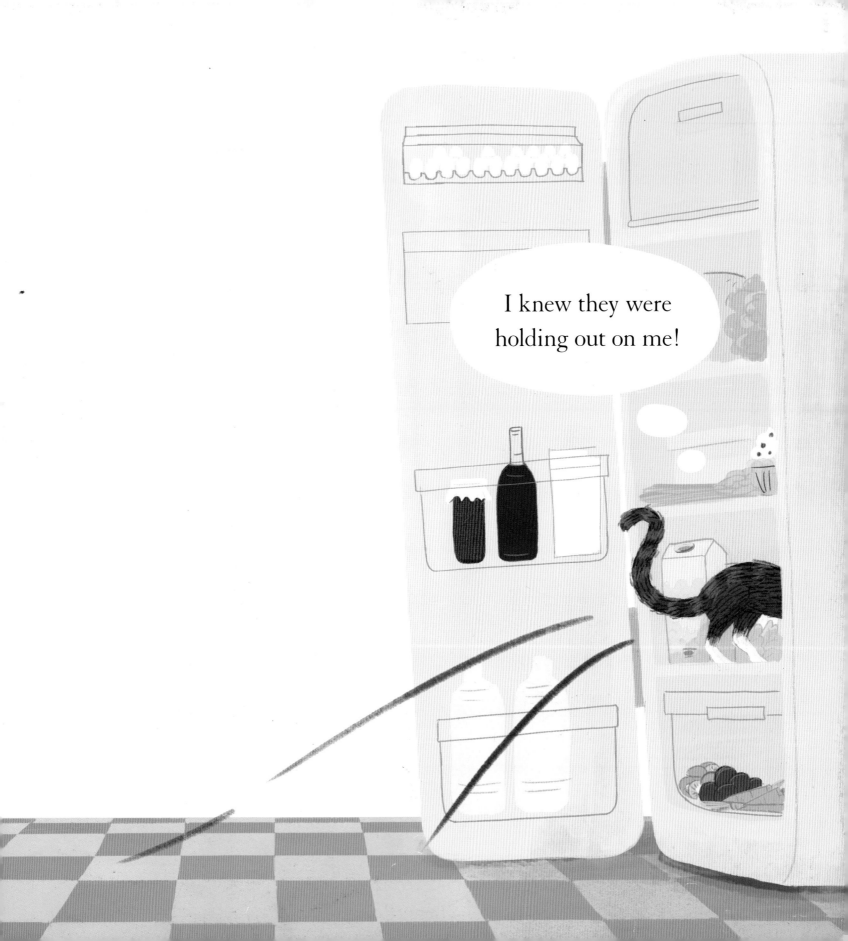